A Flower Grows

· KEN ROBBINS ·

A Flower Grows

Dial Books · New York

Published by Dial Books, A Division of Penguin Books USA Inc.
375 Hudson Street, New York, New York 10014
Published simultaneously in Canada
by Fitzhenry & Whiteside Limited, Toronto
Copyright © 1990 by Ken Robbins • All rights reserved
Design by Atha Tehon
Printed in Hong Kong by South China Printing Company (1988) Ltd.
W
First Edition
1 2 3 4 5 6 7 8 9 10

Library of Congress Cataloging in Publication Data
Robbins, Ken. A flower grows.
Summary: Illustrates the life cycle of an amaryllis.
1. Flowers — Juvenile literature. 2. Flowers — Life cycles — Juvenile literature.
3. Hippeastrum — Life cycles — Juvenile literature.
[1. Amaryllis (Hippeastrum) — Life cycles. 2. Flowers — Life cycles]
I. Title.
QK49.R64 1990   582.13′04463   89-12016
ISBN 0-8037-0764-9
ISBN 0-8037-0765-7 (lib. bdg.)

The art reproduced in this book was created from original
black-and-white photographs that were printed on ilfospeed
black-and-white paper and hand colored by the author
using water-based dyes.

This book is dedicated to Elizabeth Nina Strachan

I would like to gratefully acknowledge the highly sustaining enthusiasm of the aptly yclept Faith Hamlin, the sensitive and very significant contributions of Arthur Levine and Atha Tehon at Dial, and the generous advice and help of John Ford. Thanks also to Professor Liddle of the Southhampton College Natural Sciences Department; Abby Fleming of the Amagansett Plant Shop; Frank Robinson of the American Horticultural Society; Adriane McCoy of the Southampton College Greenhouse; Beth Calahan, my occasional assistant; and of course, Maria Polushkin, who shares her home with me and all those bulbs.

Sometimes beauty comes from the most unexpected places.
The amaryllis flower grows from an ugly thing like this:
It's the bulb of a plant called Hippeastrum.

In the wild the amaryllis grows only in tropical forests.
But indoors, gardeners anywhere can raise it for the simple
pleasure of watching as a flower grows.

They put it in a pot in the early fall. Then they nourish
it and treat it with care, and the bulb rewards their effort
first by sending up a tiny shoot of tender green.

The hollow shoot has a swollen bud on top, and grows
so quickly it's almost hard to believe — an inch and a half
or more in a day.

Gentle rain from the watering can keeps the soil soft
so that the roots can easily grow. Moisture is drawn up from
the soil, bringing food from the bulb to feed the stalk.

The rays of the sun play a crucial part in the life and growth of any plant. Sitting on a sunny window ledge, the stalk bends and arches toward the light.

Now the plant will grow and grow — eighteen inches
or more in all — until one day the bud just bursts. Inside,
hardly visible at first, are newborn flowers, all rolled up.
Slowly — just a bit each day — the delicate blossoms each
unfurl, showing off their velvety petals of lavender and pink.

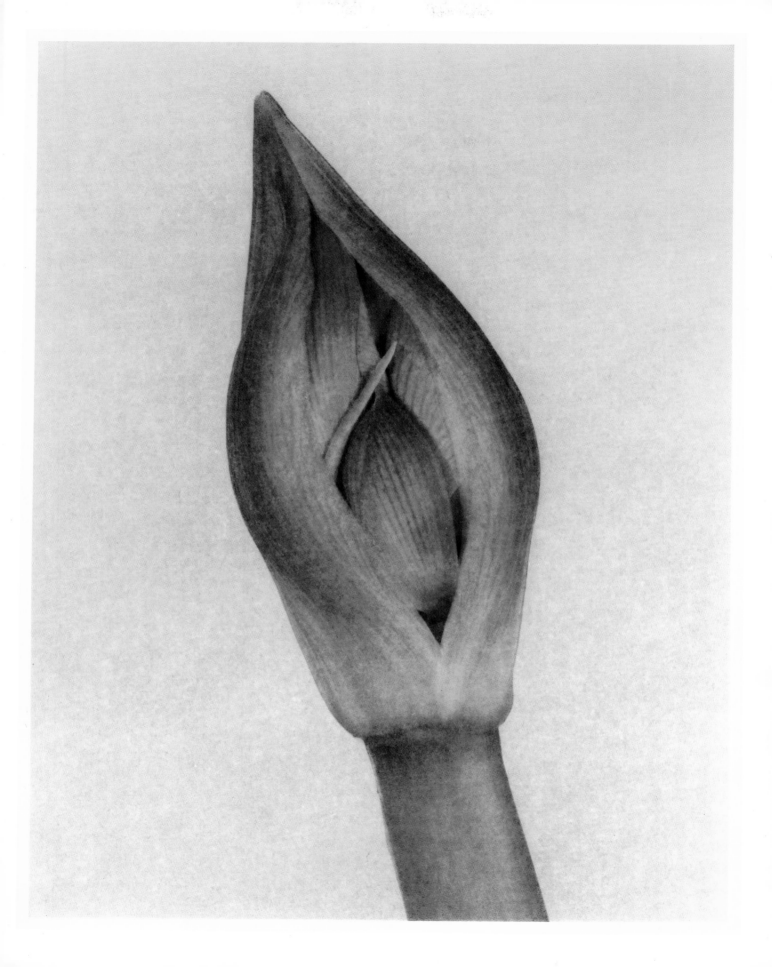

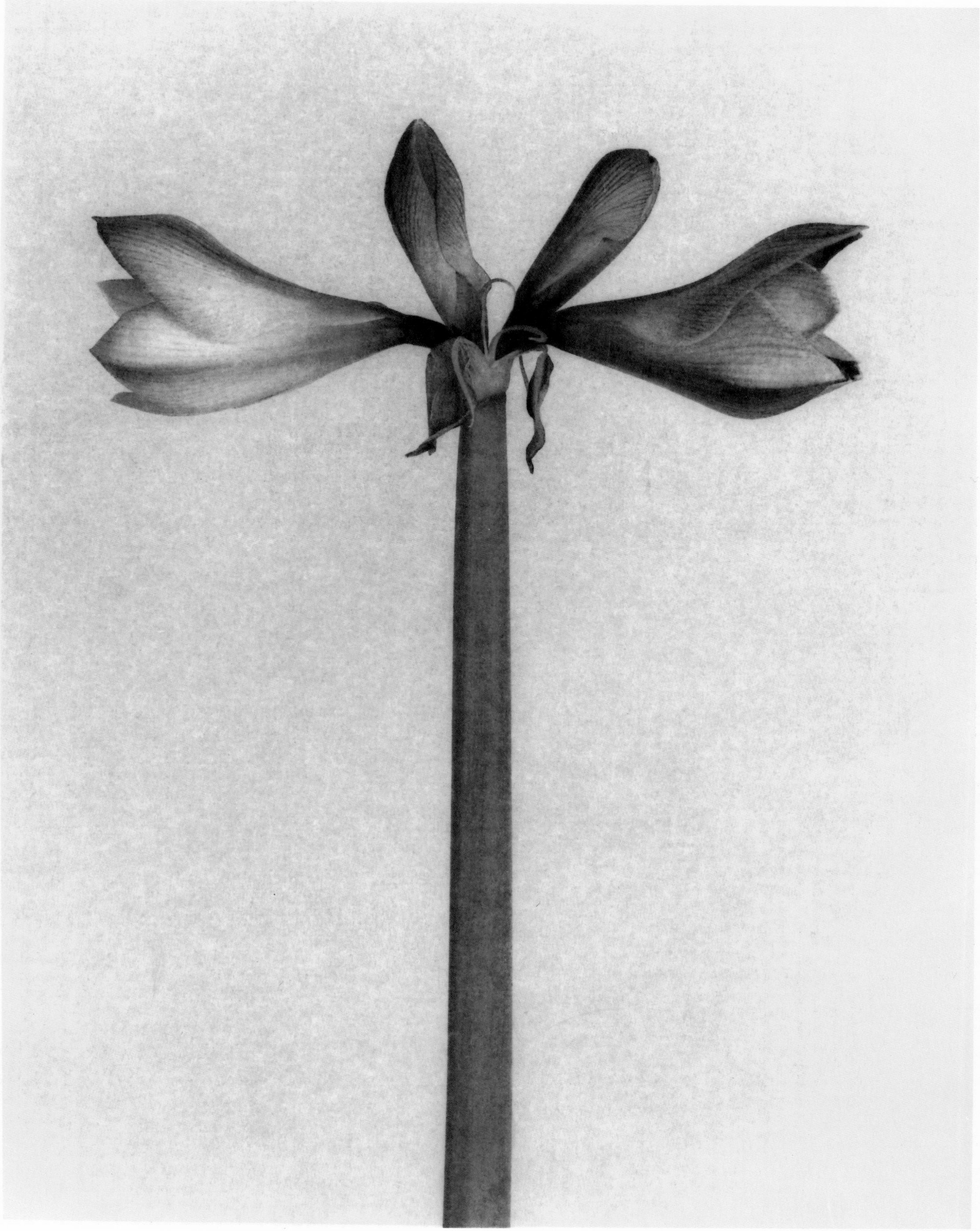

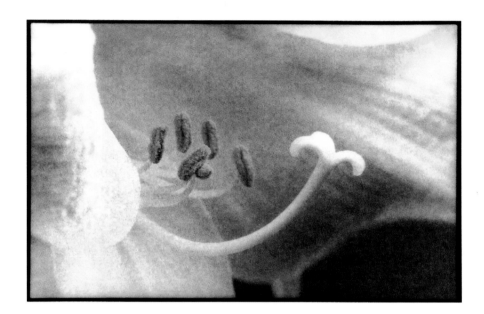

As the flowers open their petals wide, they reveal the slender, pollen-bearing stamens and the pistil with its glistening tip. These parts have the power to make the seeds that become new flowers.

Within a week or two the flowers fade and the stalk begins to wilt. Even as it does, another grows to take its place. It blooms, too, then fades away.

Eventually all the flowers die, but if they have been touched with pollen, the bases swell up fat with seeds. And if the seeds should reach some fertile ground, a whole new amaryllis plant may grow.

But even if no seeds have been produced, the plant lives on, its leaves growing up in graceful curves. The leaves produce more food, to put back in the bulb what was spent on the flower.

At last the leaves die down and when the bulb has rested,
the plant puts up a slim green stalk and a flower grows again.

Author's Note

Amaryllises are particularly hearty and dependable bulbs, and may live for ten years or more. They come in several varieties, and each blooms a different color. The one featured in this book is called Apple Blossom.

If you'd like to grow an amaryllis for yourself, early autumn is the best time to start. Get a pot about seven or eight inches deep and about eight inches across, with a drainage hole at the bottom, and a saucer to sit it on. You'll also need a small bag of potting soil, a saucer, some bone meal or other commercial fertilizer, a bag of something called pearlite, and, of course, an amaryllis bulb.

Put some pebbles in the bottom of the pot so the soil won't leak out through the drainage hole. Mix up one handful of pearlite with every four handfuls of potting soil, and fill the pot about halfway up with the mixture. Place the bulb in the pot, add more soil around the sides, and press it down gently until half the bulb is buried. Put the pot on a saucer and give it lots of water. Let it drain for a while, then pour out any extra water from the saucer.

Now let the plant rest in a warm and shady spot. Don't feed or water it until the stalk begins to emerge from the bulb. Once that happens, put your plant near a window — one that faces south if possible.

As the plant grows, the stalk bends toward the sun, so be sure to rotate the pot a quarter of a turn each day to keep it growing straight. Water it every three to four days, or whenever the soil gets dry.

After all the flowers have bloomed and faded, the long, strap-shaped leaves will begin to grow much faster. Be sure to keep watering the plant, feed it some kind of plant food or fertilizer, and keep it in a sunny spot.

When the leaves wilt and turn yellow, give the plant some food and stop watering it. Cut off the leaves at the top of the bulb and put the plant in a dark, cool, dry place to rest for several months. When you want to start it growing again, just give it some water, put it in a warm spot, and let nature take its course.